A HAPPY NEW YEAR'S DAY

© 1991 Roch Carrier: text
© 1991 Gilles Pelletier: illustrations

The original version of *A Happy New Year's Day* was published in the Montreal *Gazette*, under the title ''Remembrance of a New Year's Repast,'' on December 31, 1988.

Published in Canada by Tundra Books, Montreal, Quebec H3G 1R4

Published in the United States by Tundra Books of Northern New York, Plattsburgh, N.Y. 12901

Library of Congress Catalog Number: 91-65367

Distributed in France by Le Colporteur Diffusion, 63110 Beaumont

Canadian Cataloging in Publication Data:

Carrier, Roch, 1937-

[Bonne et heureuse année. English]
   A Happy New Year's Day
ISBN 0-88776-267-0

(Issued also in French under title: *Une bonne et heureuse année*. ISBN 0-88776-268-9)

I. Pelletier, Gilles, 1946- . II. Title. III. Title: Bonne et heureuse année. English.

PS8505.A77C6613 1991   C843'.54   C91-090259-3
PZ7.C37Ha 1991

Design by Dan O'Leary

Printed in Hong Kong by South China Printing Co. Ltd.

A HAPPY NEW YEAR'S DAY

Text by Roch Carrier

Illustrations by Gilles Pelletier

 Tundra Books

May I tell you about New Year's Day, 1941? Why this particular one? Because it's the first one I can remember. Before that day, to me, the world did not really exist. On that day, everything started to be. So here is the story of the beginning of my world.

It was not an easy time on earth, but in my village, at the border between Quebec and the U.S., I was not aware of this. I was four years old.

My parents listened to the news on the radio many times a day. I was much more interested in the little lamps with their sparks inside the wooden cabinet. I spent long hours, behind the radio, trying to understand the mystery of the talking.

My parents read the paper carefully. How could those dots covering the paper like small insects also talk to my parents? All I could read were the photographs.

On the front page, soldiers were carrying guns, like the men in my village did during the hunting season. How did I discover that their guns were not for bears or for moose?

It was later that I understood that kids of my age, in Europe, were hiding in cold places, starving, to avoid persecution or running to hide from bombs. I had not yet discovered that the world is not always a fair place to be.

But I'm anticipating. Let's go back to the very beginning of my story, in August, 1940. Why August? Because that was the month my grandmother picked the cherries for the New Year's Day wine.

I accompanied her in the fields, then watched her make the wine. She filled many cooking-pots with cherries. I helped her, removing worms, insects, leaves.

I was asked to stir the boiling broth. The sweet steam was so delicious! I inhaled the way my father smoked. Suddenly I fell on my bottom. I didn't cry. I was kind of sleepy. My grandmother said, "The little rascal likes wine; aren't you ashamed?" She picked me up in her arms, she pressed me against her and laughed and laughed as if I had made a funny joke.

The summer was not over and my grandmother was bottling wine for New Year's Day. As I realized later, that was the only day wine was permitted in her house. Before and after this very special day, wine – even the wine she made – was the devil's invention, a curse that affected families.

On the wall of her kitchen hung a large black cross. It was a symbol of the oath my grandparents had made to the parish priest: no liquor, not even cherry wine, would be drunk except on the very special occasion that was New Year's Day.

September came. The big children left for school. I stayed home with the adults. I kept busy visiting the farmers and helping them. Farmers always need help.

After the heavy work of the harvest, they would get their sleighs ready for winter. They repaired the leather upholstered seats. They painted or varnished the sleighs. I still can see their big hands painting the sleighs with exquisite garlands of painted flowers.

In December my mother and my grandmother started baking meat pies we called tourtières and pies filled with maple sugar, strawberry jam, raspberry jam. They were also busy rolling in their hands cookies, chocolate, candies. All those goodies were carefully stored in the cold room. My mother locked the door and she carried the key in her apron pocket.

Snow would pile up. The villagers who owned cars kept them in a garage or barn. The road was not cleared of snow. Instead, a giant roller, pulled by three farm horses, compressed and hardened the snow. Thus the village remained purely white.

For Christmas, under the tree decorated with colorful balls and silver paper icicles, there was the beautiful crèche that my father built with small dry branches. Baby Jesus was accompanied by plaster cattle, sheep and donkeys. The straw was real. There was a scream when I found baby Jesus in our cat's mouth. He had to surrender under the attacks of all my brothers and sisters, who all wanted to save Jesus.

I was too small to attend midnight mass. In my bed, I could at least listen to the bells on the horses' harness. I barely slept. The real baby Jesus was being born during that night and I was as anxious as when a baby was being born into our family.

At last New Year's Day came! I got up early to see my gift. My sisters and brothers were ahead of me. Under the tree, there was a red locomotive for me: It was my dream come true. I had discovered how magical the train was one day when father took me to the station. There was noise, smoke. The earth shook under my feet. A black man, something I had seen only in a missionary magazine, waved at me with a wide smile on his white teeth.

E ach time I heard the whistling train arriving at our station, I danced with joy. I just loved the voice of the train. Once my father said, "This boy of mine will not remain with us in the village."

But now, I had my own locomotive, a red one! I was a four-year-old boy and the only thing I knew was that this red locomotive was mine. My mother took a photograph of her proud son. I'm smiling like one who believes everybody is happy.

After having enjoyed the toys, we were told to dress up to go to my grandparents' for New Year's dinner.

My father was the privileged owner of a snowmobile. This vehicle looked like a strange plane. It was on skis – it had no wings. The propeller at the back could push the snowmobile ahead at an impressive speed. The rumbling sound it made was still more remarkable. It was like thunder. The windows vibrated, the dishes in the cupboards shook, when my father's snowmobile was on its way.

Our house was 200 feet from my grandparents'. We walked that distance many times a day. On New Year's Day it was different. It was a day for pomp, flamboyance. My father decided to pile us into his snowmobile.

We were looking through the small windows. He started the machine. Hearing the thunder so close, the horses jumped, pranced and ran away with their sleighs full of frightened families. My father said to my mother: "Pray God that He does not punish my sin of pride by sending accidents to innocent people."

Nobody in the village could be unaware that our family was going to visit our grandparents for New Year's dinner. During that short trip I really felt as if I were the little prince of the whole planet.

My grandmother's kitchen was warmly perfumed by what was cooking. The wood stove was covered with frying pans, cooking pots, cauldrons. Covers were flapping in the steam. The kitchen was full of uncles, aunts, cousins, crawling babies and girls with colored ribbons in their hair.

There was a lot of kissing. "Happy New Year!" Against my will, I flew from uncles to aunts. My face was rubbed by sharp beards and licked by lips as I was crushed against chests. Some of the family came from a faraway town, at least 30 miles from our place.

Unknown people arrived with us: "Happy New Year! We wish you a very good health because it's better than money!"

"I wish you the holy paradise at the end of your days! May it be the latest possible!"

The new people were well-wishers going from house to house. My grandfather offered them a glass of cherry wine. I understood that at every house they visited they were accepting something to drink.

My grandmother invited the family to sit down at the table. She checked that everybody had a place, a chair, a plate. She did not want to hurt anybody's feelings by a miscalculation. All was good. She announced: "Now, it's time for the paternal benediction."

We all knelt down. According to the tradition, the father should bless his children on the New Year's Day. My grandfather said: "This year, Grandma will give you the paternal benediction." My grandmother stood up and pronounced the traditional words.

I listened to the whispers and I understood that my grandfather had become too shy. He was a very simple man, a carpenter. He had never attended school.

Suddenly he had realized that his daughters were all school teachers. One of his sons was studying Latin to become a priest and probably a bishop. His other sons had piles of books in their rooms. One of them even knew how to speak English. My grandfather felt unfit for speaking in front of his educated children.

After my grandmother blessed us, she filled the glasses with her cherry wine. "Let's drink to our good health! Happy New Year!"

My grandmother did not drink. She only sniffed the bouquet and immediately declared: "I'm drunk!" and started laughing. But everybody was also laughing at seeing my grandmother laughing.

My mother explained to me: "Grandma gets happy when she smells her cherry wine." At the other end of the table, my grandfather was blushing.

Some seconds later, my grandmother, very serious, was filling our plates with turkey meat, pigs' knuckles, tourtière, meatballs, vegetables, green tomato ketchup.

The grown-ups were talking about cows and horses, dead people, the province's premier, babies to come, babies just arrived. They were having so much pleasure, talking together, all at the same time. I got bored and went to the window.

On the only street of the village, under the shining sun, there was a brilliant parade of sleighs. The horses were vigorous, well brushed; they were proud in their fancy harnesses. They played music with their bells. In the colorful sleighs, the families were wrapped in fur and scarves.

The door opened and a small old lady, all dressed in black like a widow, appeared. "Happy New Year to all of you, cousins, grand-cousins and so on!" she shouted. "I'm so tired. I did not sleep. I was in my bed, last night, alone. My husband died seventeen months ago. It was silent but I heard sobs behind the wall.

"I also heard steps on the floor. I heard somebody sitting down in my husband's chair, where he used to smoke his pipe. I knew that my husband was coming back from the cemetery for New Year's Day.

"I said to him: 'My husband, stop crying. When one is dead, one is dead.' Poor man..."

"Poor Anna," said my grandmother, "have a glass of cherry wine."

"Give me one for my husband too. It is so sad to have to spend New Year's Day alone in a cemetery."

"New Year's Day is not a day to be sad. Drink Anna!"

And then it was time for dessert.

Plates were being distributed with maple sugar pie, apple pie, Christmas log cake, *sucre à la crème* – all covered with fresh cream.

All together, as if thrown off their chairs, everybody knelt down. I did the same. It was the parish priest:

"I come to bring you God's blessing. May the New Year prepare you to enter His Kingdom." He traced some signs of the Holy Cross in the air. Everybody imitated him. I did too.

"Husband," said my grandmother, "give a jug of cherry wine to our priest."

The priest held it like a baby against his chest. "Thank you," he said. "By chance, my sexton is following me with a sleigh. Otherwise, I would be unable to carry all the gifts my pious parishioners are giving me. Giving to your priest is giving to God."

An uncle could not come because he was living as far away as Montreal.

My grandfather told his son, the priest-to-be, "You must be able to dial for long distance." My uncle the priest-to-be turned the little crank, put the receiver to his ear and shouted into the mouthpiece. "They are answering," he announced.

We all felt a miracle was happening.

Everybody rushed to the telephone. Everbody yelled his message, her news, to my uncle and my aunt who were living so far away. I started to yell too. I did it with such conviction that I was lifted to the telephone.

"I hope you don't want to drive your Grandpa to bankruptcy with a too-expensive long distance phone call," said my grandmother.

Then she announced: "Children, here is the moment for your presents!"

In a lot of wrappings feverishly torn apart, there were knitted socks and sweaters, gloves, ties and toys.

What did I receive? I forgot. However, I remember precisely that the gift came in a shoe box.

With my young uncle's help, I converted the shoe box into a sleigh. I caught the cat, a big tom cat with brownish fur; I attached the shoe box to its neck and the cat became my horse.

Engrossed in my game, sheltered under the table, I didn't notice the arrival of a violinist and an accordionist. Music started. The table was pushed against the wall. The chairs were taken to the shed to make room for the dancers. A fat aunt picked me up and she danced, holding me against her warm bosom and kissing me. I managed to escape.

All the coats were piled up in a room. Most of them were fur coats. There was a mountain of fur coats. I climbed and I found a cavern where I could get in and hide from other aunts that were threatening to kiss me. I crawled into my fur cave. I soon fell asleep.

They found me many hours later. It was night. Many wine jugs were sitting on the table. There were also many bottles of beer with the little black horse I loved so much on the label. The uncles' shirts were all wet. The exhausted aunts were not even talking. The music seemed sad. The day had come to an end.

My mother dressed me up in my white rabbit fur coat, my white rabbit fur hat; my grandmother helped her to dress the babies; my father carried us to his snowmobile. With the sound of thunder, he drove us home.

The propeller stopped whipping the air. Silence descended on the illuminated village.

"I wish us all a very happy New Year!" said my father.

"I wish you very good health because you have a big family to take care of," answered my mother.

"I wish you a new baby," said my father.

"I wish our kids that we make them happy all year round like they were happy today," said my mother.

"Don't say that because they will remember when you have to tell them off," said my father.

"Children forget everything," said my mother.

We got out of the snowmobile. In the night, billion-year-old stars looked brand new.

I shouted to the sky, "Happy New Year, God!"

Over the last twenty-five years **Roch Carrier** has taught, lectured and, most importantly, written some of the most beloved books to come out of Quebec. The author of such well-known works as *La guerre, Yes Sir!*, and the children's classic *The Hockey Sweater*, Carrier's work continues to be widely read in both its original French and in English. He has lectured extensively in Canada, the United States, England, Europe and Australia and has recently written the text for *Canada je t'aime/I love you*, a collaboration with painter Miyuki Tanobe. He has served on many cultural boards and was the Chairman of Montreal's Salon du Livre for several years. *A Happy New Year's Day* takes place in Sainte-Justine, the small village of Roch's childhood near the Quebec/Maine border, that has inspired so many of his other works, including *The Hockey Sweater* and *The Boxing Champion*.

Inspired by the traditions of the great folk artists of the United States, **Gilles Pelletier** started painting on found objects, farm implements and antiques. He also sculpts wooden ducks, horses, pigs and cows, and is an avid collector and restorer of antiques. Although his formal paintings have grown in size and complexity in recent years, they still reflect the color and charm of country life – making him a particularly appropriate illustrator for Carrier's joyous New Year's story. Pelletier lives amidst his many antiques and cats in Ormstown, Quebec, south of Montreal.